Clockwork Mouse's Wish

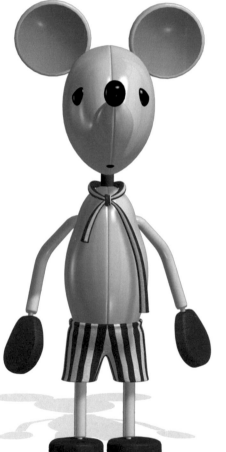

HarperCollins *Children's Books*

It was a lovely day in Toyland and Noddy was giving Clockwork Mouse a lift in his taxi.

"Thanks for the ride, Noddy," said Clockwork Mouse. "Can you drop me off at Dinah Doll's stall?"

As Clockwork Mouse began to get out of the car,
his spring started to wind down.

"Thank you so-o-o m-u-u-ch," Clockwork
mouse said, "Uh-oh… I ne-e-e-e-ed wi-i-i-i-nding…"

Noddy reached over and turned Clockwork
Mouse's key.

"Thank you, Noddy," said Clockwork Mouse,
happily. "When my spring runs down, I always need
someone to turn my key."

"I'm glad to help," said Noddy. "Especially since your key is so little – it's easy to turn."

"How much do I owe you for the taxi ride, Noddy?" Clockwork Mouse asked.

"Nothing!" chirped Noddy. "I'm happy to give you a ride for free. I know if I was as small as you, I would enjoy a ride once in a while!"

"Oh, um… thanks…" Clockwork Mouse frowned as he left the car.

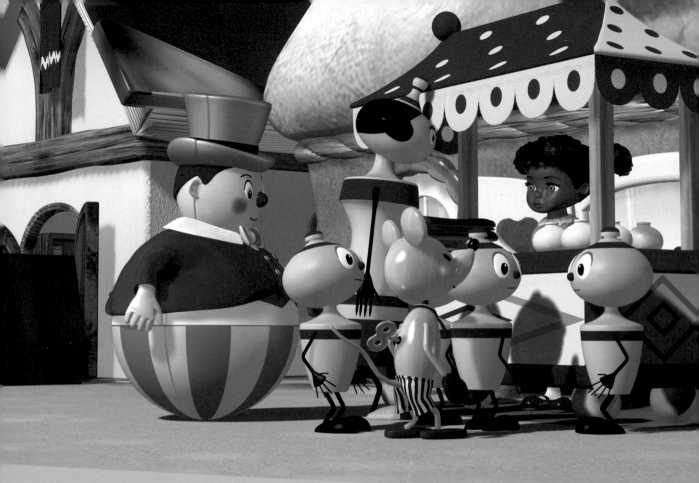

The Skittle children were crowding around Dinah Doll's stall.

"Uh, Dinah Doll," said Clockwork Mouse, trying to get her attention. "Excuse me."

"Skittles, please!" shouted Mrs Skittle, not noticing Clockwork Mouse. "Will you children be quiet? I'm trying to talk to Dinah Doll."

"Excuse me, Mrs Skittle," interrupted Clockwork Mouse. "I am not one of your children."

"No," chuckled Mr Wobbly Man, "but you're small enough to look like one of them!"

Mr Wobbly Man broke into a hearty laugh and almost wobbled right into Clockwork Mouse.

"Hey!" Clockwork Mouse shouted. "Be careful!"

Dinah Doll looked down and noticed
Clockwork Mouse.

"Oh, I'm sorry," Dinah Doll said. "I didn't see
you down there. I'll be with you in a moment."

"Nevermind. I'll come back later," muttered
Clockwork Mouse. "When there aren't so many
BIG folk around."

Noddy was whizzing past in his car and almost didn't notice Clockwork Mouse trying to cross the road.

Parp! Parp!

"I'm sorry, Clockwork Mouse," Noddy said. "I didn't see you down there!"

"It seems like NOBODY ever sees me!" replied Clockwork Mouse.

"Would you like a lift somewhere else?" Noddy asked.

"Yes, I think I would like to visit my best friend, Mr Jumbo," said Clockwork Mouse, sadly.

Noddy and Clockwork Mouse pulled up to
Mr Jumbo's house.

"Here we are, Clockwork Mouse," said Noddy,
happily. "See, it wasn't that far."

"Maybe not for you, Noddy, but EVERYWHERE
is far when you have legs a little as mine," replied
Clockwork Mouse.

"Well, if you aren't going to stay long, I could
wait for you?" Noddy offered, kindly.

"Thank you, Noddy," Clockwork Mouse replied.
"That would be nice."

Mr Jumbo was watering the plants in his garden.
Clockwork Mouse scuttled over to see
his best friend.

"Hello, Mr Jumbo," said Clockwork
Mouse, quietly.

"Oh, hello, Clockwork Mouse!"
Mr Jumbo replied. "How are you?"

"I'm not feeling very good today," said Clockwork Mouse, quietly. "I'm tired of being small."

Mr Jumbo bent down to speak to his friend. "Why do you think you're small?" he asked, peering down at Clockwork Mouse.

"Because everyone bends over when they talk to me!" said Clockwork Mouse. "Even you!"

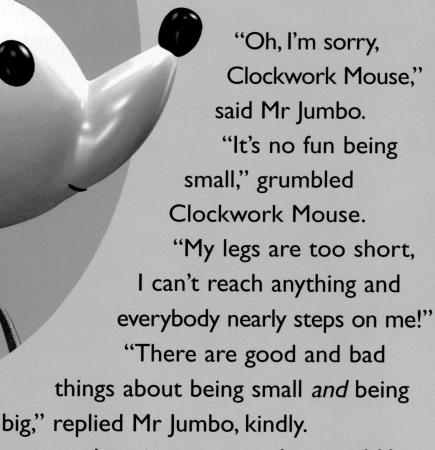

"Oh, I'm sorry,
Clockwork Mouse,"
said Mr Jumbo.
"It's no fun being
small," grumbled
Clockwork Mouse.
"My legs are too short,
I can't reach anything and
everybody nearly steps on me!"
"There are good and bad
things about being small *and* being
big," replied Mr Jumbo, kindly.
"It doesn't matter what size you are. Anyway, I like
you just the way you are!"
"What? Look at me!" cried Clockwork Mouse. "I'm
hardly bigger than Bumpy Dog! I wish people would
pay attention-n-n to-o-o-o me-e-e-e-e..."

Clockwork Mouse had started to wind down again.
Mr Jumbo picked him up and turned his little key.

"Thank you, Mr Jumbo," said Clockwork Mouse.
"And thanks for listening."

"That's what friends are for, Clockwork Mouse."
Mr Jumbo smiled.

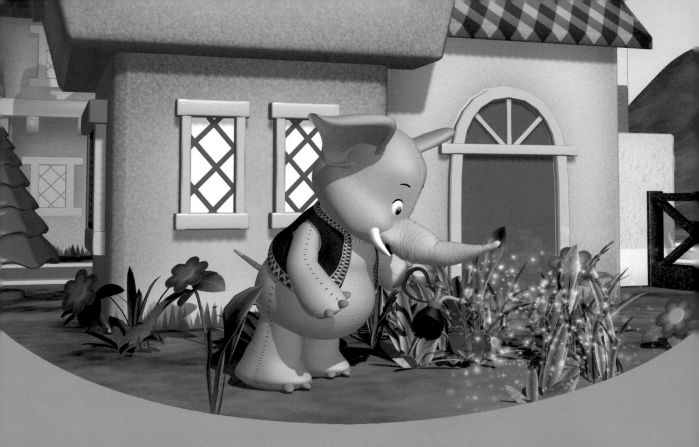

Mr Jumbo then started to sprinkle some colourful plant food onto his flowers. The small flowers suddenly grew and blossomed, giving Clockwork Mouse quite a shock.

"How do you do that?!" asked Clockwork Mouse, excitedly.

"Oh, it's special plant food I made up," Mr Jumbo replied, proudly. "It makes very small flowers as big as the other ones. Isn't it amazing?"

"If it can make plants grow, maybe it can make ME grow!" thought Clockwork Mouse.

As soon as Mr Jumbo went indoors, Clockwork Mouse grabbed his special plant food and sprinkled it all over his little body.

Suddenly, he started to grow!

"Wow!" he thought, happily. "Now I'm as tall as Noddy!"

Noddy was still waiting outside Mr Jumbo's house when Clockwork Mouse came to say hello.

"Back to town, please, Noddy!" Clockwork Mouse said, happily.

Noddy looked at Clockwork Mouse strangely. "Are you alright? You seem different somehow."

"No, everything is just fine!" Clockwork Mouse said, with a smile.

Clockwork Mouse wanted to show off his new size
to all his friends. First stop was the Town Square
to see Martha Monkey.

"Hello, Martha Monkey!" shouted Clockwork
Mouse. "Notice anything different about me?"

"Yes," Martha Monkey giggled. "You've got pink ears!"

"No! Can't you see I'm taller?" Clockwork
Mouse replied.

"Maybe a little... but not taller than me!"
said Martha Monkey, standing up straight.

"I'm still not big enough!" thought Clockwork
Mouse. "I need more special plant food."

With that, he jumped back into Noddy's
car and asked Noddy to take him back
to Mr Jumbo's house.

As soon as he arrived, he ran behind
Mr Jumbo's house and sprinkled the
whole pot of special plant food
all over himself!

"Now I'm bigger than Martha Monkey, bigger than Mr Wobbly Man and bigger than Mr Jumbo!" cried Clockwork Mouse.

This time, Clockwork Mouse had grown so tall, he was bigger than Mr Jumbo's house!

"Oh dear, Mouse!" Noddy cried, as he came round the corner. "Look how big you are! What have you been doing?"

"I want to show everyone how big I am, Noddy," said Clockwork Mouse, happily. "Please drive me back to town!"

"I can't! You're too big for my car," replied Noddy.

"So I am!" Clockwork Mouse said, proudly. "Now I've got big legs, I can walk to town quickly!"

"Make way, everyone!" Noddy cried as they set off. "Here comes a giant!"

"Look, everyone! I'm not smaller than you!
I am bigger than EVERYTHING!" shouted
Clockwork Mouse.

Clockwork Mouse walked over to see
Miss Pink Cat. "Miss Pink Cat! I'd like a LARGE
ice cream, now!"

Miss Pink Cat was making ice cream inside
her ice cream parlour.

"Oh!" cried Miss Pink Cat, when she poked
her head of the window. "Um… here you go!"

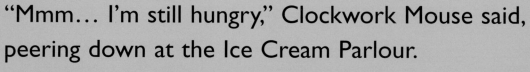

"Mmm… I'm still hungry," Clockwork Mouse said, peering down at the Ice Cream Parlour. "Could I have a hundred more, please?"

"Well, that will cost you about a hundred coins, Mr Mouse," stammered Miss Pink Cat.

"I don't have that much money," replied Clockwork Mouse. "Oh well, I don't need ice cream! And I don't need taxis! I can walk across town in a few steps!"

And so Clockwork
Mouse took a huge step
and knocked right into the police station.

"Goodness me!" Mr Plod shouted, when
he saw Clockwork Mouse causing chaos. "I don't
care if you are a giant, you put my police station
back where it belongs, right now!"

"I'm sorry, Mr Plod," said Clockwork Mouse,
taking a step backwards.

"I should put you in jail!" Mr Plod replied, angrily.
"If you could fit, that is!"

"OK, I'm leaving now," Clockwork Mouse said,
trying to walk away without causing any more trouble.

Without thinking, Clockwork Mouse turned
around and nearly stepped on Dinah Doll.

"Watch out, Clockwork Mouse!" shouted Dinah Doll.

"Run away, everyone! This giant mouse may step
on you!" cried
Mr Wobbly Man.

"I don't mean to!" Clockwork Mouse said,
looking around for help. "I need Noddy!
Where is Noddy?"

Clockwork Mouse crashed into Noddy's house.

"Oops! Noddy, are you in there?" Clockwork
Mouse said, peering into Noddy's house.
"Help me, Noddy! I don't like being big anymore.
I can't buy ice cream. I can't ride in your car. Everyone
is afraid of me! Plus, my spring is wi-i-i-nn-d-ing-ng-ng
downnnn-n-n-n-n. . ."

"Sorry, Mouse, but nobody can wind you up again," explained Noddy. "You're just too big!"

Mr Jumbo ran over to Clockwork Mouse with a potion in his hand.

"Don't worry, Clockwork Mouse," cried Mr Jumbo. "I have a potion that I use to make weeds smaller. Maybe it will work on you, too!"

Gradually, Clockwork Mouse began to shrink.

Smaller

and smaller

and smaller.

Soon he was back to his usual small self. "You saved me, Mr Jumbo!" Clockwork Mouse said, happily. "Thank you! Being tall is not as much fun as I thought it would be."

"We are sorry," said Mr Wobbly Man. "We didn't realise how sad you were, being small."

"I promise to pay attention to you when you come to my stall," said Dinah Doll, kindly.

"I'll still give you free taxi rides!" Noddy chimed.

"And free ice cream!" chirped Miss Pink Cat.

"You know, there are good things about
being small, after all!" giggled Clockwork Mouse.
"I'll say!" said Noddy.

An ant, a whale, a horse, a snail,
Who cares if we are short or tall,
Big or small?
A bear, a bee, and you, and me,
We're simply perfect, one and all,
Big or small!